MIRANDA'S
SILVER SHOES

Story and photographs:
Judith Ratcliffe

Front cover design:
Christina Ratcliffe

ARTHUR H. STOCKWELL LTD
Torrs Park   Ilfracombe   Devon
Established 1898
www.ahstockwell.co.uk

British Library Cataloguing-in-Publication Data.
A catalogue record for this book is available
from the British Library.

ISBN 978-0-7223-4972-4
Printed in Great Britain by
Arthur H. Stockwell Ltd
Torrs Park   Ilfracombe
Devon EX34 8BA

CHAPTER 1

It is a sad thing that most adults have forgotten how to do magic. The hard world of work and disappointed dreams crushes it out of them, as surely as a paper cup can be crushed under the heel of a shoe.

Luckily, the odd one or two, secretly, still do, though they will never admit it if you ask them. You will know who they are by the way they smile, and the sparkle in their eyes.

One of those few is Miranda. Miranda was a person who was frequently scolded for jumping in puddles with her best pair of shoes on, who would stand outside in a snow shower just to catch the flakes as they fell down, wondering at the patterns on her ungloved hand.

She came across it by accident one day, when riding her bicycle along by the canal to get to work.

It was a beautiful sunrise that day – the clouds were purple and the sun was a golden orb, sending red stripes across the sky.

Her eyes followed the path of a kingfisher to a tree, where there was a great hole in the middle of the trunk. There, in the darkness, something glistened.

Curiosity caused her to stop the bike so suddenly, it skidded on the gravel and she nearly fell off. Leaning it against the nearby hedgerow, fragrant with the beautiful blossoms of springtime and singing with bees and sparrows, she climbed the fence next to the tree and stretched up on tiptoe to reach into the hole in the tree.

An angry 'chak chak' met her ears, and she quickly withdrew her hand as a squirrel appeared at the entrance to the hole, preparing to nip any fingers intruding into its home. It moved its tail backwards and forwards, daring the young woman to come any closer, and then, turning its back, began to scuff the inside of its home.

As it scuffed, it knocked the shining thing to one side in such a way that the shining thing overbalanced and toppled into the surprised creature. A screech of annoyance from the squirrel followed – attacks from inside its home were highly irregular and not to be borne lightly, and it decided to avenge itself on the glistening thing by using all its might to push it back. The thing fell from the hole, almost hitting our heroine on the head as she sat on the fence, trying to work out how to retrieve it without being bitten by a pack of mad squirrels.

The glistening thing was a shoe. And, what is more, it was a shoe that she recognised.

It was a magic shoe.

And she also knew that things would never be the same again.

CHAPTER 2

The shoe was worn and old and silver, with purple laces and a heel half fallen off, with the odd nibble mark here and there, where the squirrels had obviously decided that even a shoe, in the middle of winter, when your store of nuts is running low, is better than freezing feet in the icy world outside your snug nest.

Miranda tucked it into the top of her rucksack and continued, whistling, on her way.

She wondered what had become of the other shoe, and was not surprised when a rather unusual parcel appeared on her desk mid-afternoon. No one knew who had brought it in or signed for it and it would not be her birthday for many months. There was no label and it was really only a cardboard shoebox with an elastic band round it, but the treasure it hid inside was making it shake with energy, with all the adventures it had seen.

When she lifted the lid, she found the partner of the shoe gifted her by the squirrel on the canal.

Of course, then she couldn't wait to get home and try them on.

It was raining hard all evening, and by the time she got home she was drenched to the skin. Taking her rucksack off and leaving it in the hall, while she went upstairs to get changed, she didn't notice the strange, unearthly glow which was coming from the bag where she now had both silver shoes.

She couldn't help a grin, though, when she opened the bag, a few minutes later, and took out, not two worn, nibbled old shoes, half falling to bits, as they had been before, but two glowing, new-looking and just-the-right-size-for-her shoes.

She put them on straight away and spun round in them, once, for luck.

Just then, there was an almighty flash of light and a great roar which shook the entire house.

People in the surrounding area just thought it was the storm passing overhead, but our heroine knew better than that.

CHAPTER 3

The words came to her in an instant. She closed her eyes and with one finger wrote her name across the stars.

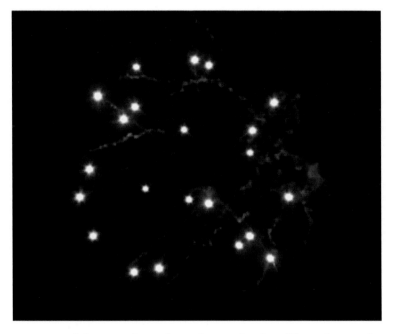

Then she peered into the depths of the Earth and opened up her ears to hear beyond the rain.

There she stood in her Silver Shoes, underneath the stars, reaching out with her mind, searching for answers, touching magic with the tips of her fingers, letting it lick round them like flame.

And then she saw it, in a clearing – a dragon – sitting toasting sausages, holding a fork out in front of its own flame, and, when they were properly burnt, swallowing them whole.

When it had finished, it packed everything up into a small knapsack, as all environmentally conscious dragons do, and fell asleep at the foot of a giant oak tree, puffing out smoke rings as it snored.

There had been a small clump of bushes in the clearing. This now vanished, reappearing as a small band of trolls – trolls who were grinning mischievously and whispering to one another and pointing at the sleeping dragon, chattering with excitement.

This particular band of trolls lived in a series of tunnels dug from the main one that they had found in the wall of the castle on the hill at the edge of town.

They looked a bit like overgrown hedgehogs with fur where the spikes should be, very flat, clumpy feet, big hands, pointed elfin ears and beady black eyes, which flashed and turned yellow in the dark of their tunnel den.

They were mostly nocturnal, as you can get up to mischief much more easily when no one else can see you, or, at least, this lot tried to get up to mischief, but usually ended up falling over each other in the dark, or casting spells on each other instead . . . and so the world was, by and large, spared their menaces.

Spared, that is, until they found the dragon, and an unusually bright member of that little gang of troll-scouts had a thought. . . .

And the thought grew into an idea. . . .

And the idea became a plan that soon had the whole lot of them making muffled squeaks of excitement – squeaks that said "a pet dragon", "a dragon whose power we can take", "is a dragon good to eat?"

Squeaks of horror and indignation followed that last thought, for, as you know, dragons are scaly creatures and their armour plating makes them highly undesirable as food, even to the most starving and desperate of creatures.

But here we must pause in our account of the fate of the dragon, for the Silver Shoes had other ideas to begin with.

They took their new owner off the ground, flying over the houses and landing in the garden of The Great Magician.

CHAPTER 4

It was unusual for The Great Magician to have a garden, as you will know from other stories concerning Yellow Ted, Badger and the Magic Ring, for usually The Great Magician lives in a cave.

However, true to form, in one sense at least, on this occasion, The Great Magician opened the back door that led into his garden. He said 'Ye-e-es?' in his usual very deep voice and looked at Miranda over the top of his spectacles.

Miranda looked down at her shoes, back up at The Great Magician, decided that the person standing at his back door in a pair of very old slippers and a very pointy hat with stars and moons on it was probably a friendly sort, and, having made her decision, extended an equally friendly hand.

The Shoes, at that point, thinking that they must have been overlooked, and not liking to be overlooked, gave a magical shimmer and twinkled so brightly you could almost hear them.

'Ah, yes, there you are,' The Great Magician said, finally looking at the Shoes and really talking more to himself than to them. 'Well, I suppose you had better come in.'

The Shoes tapped themselves in an 'I should think so' sort of way, which thoroughly surprised the current wearer, who you will remember was Miranda, and very nearly tripped her over.

'I do hope you take better care of this one,' The Great Magician continued. 'Leaving your last owner at the mercy of that *Tyrannosaurus rex* might perhaps be considered a step too far, if you will excuse the . . .' He trailed off, as the Shoes flashed a dangerous hint of red. 'All right,' – he held up his hands – 'I was only saying. Now then, young lady,' – he appeared to notice Miranda, at last – 'I gather that you have come to see me about a band of trolls.'

'Not exactly. I—'

Miranda heard a very loud purr behind her that could not possibly belong to any ordinary cat, and prayed that the thing that was now walking round her legs, and that was clearly a lot bigger than an ordinary cat, had already been fed.

For self-preservation purposes, she made up her mind to nod and smile and follow The Great Magician, until she could escape back the way she had come.

The Shoes clearly agreed with at least half of this sentiment. They quickly pulled Miranda through a door into a courtyard, in the middle of which was a huge crystal ball mounted on a plinth.

When she saw it, she stopped and stared.

Inside the crystal ball shapes were moving about – blurry, fuzzy shapes at first, until The Great Magician moved a coat hanger on the front of a wardrobe in the corner of the room 'to get a better signal'.

The blurry, fuzzy shapes moved together, separated and vanished with a crackle, and then . . .

There were the trolls. You and I met them earlier, but Miranda had not, so she still did not know what they were.

Two of them scampered up a tree with a rope they seemed to have magicked out of thin air.

They lowered it carefully, slowly, until it was just next to the dragon's snout.

There was a muffled squeak as they missed lassoing it from above, once, twice . . .

The third time, they were lucky.

The dragon woke with a mighty puff of smoke and a splutter through its nostrils – no fire, no sound.

It was trussed like a turkey and being rather roughly bumped along the path by the trolls, who had decided, as even all together the dragon was too heavy to lift, to roll it back to their lair.

When they were, after much pushing and shoving, in the darkness once more, deep underneath the castle, they pushed the dragon into a corner. Those who had not made up the scouting party came forward and poked at it and peered at it, and ended up sitting on it and looking up expectantly at the others, waiting for an explanation.

The self-acclaimed leader pulled himself up to his full miniature size and, when that wasn't big enough, climbed on top of the troll next to him to make himself twice his usual size.

'Troll needs dragon magic.

Fire to burn village - make peoples run round, forget to guard food stores.

Magic to shrink peoples.

Grow trolls big.

Slave peoples.

Peoples cook for trolls.

Big snack-time!

Make peoples run big wheel - get water for power troll water slide.

Make trolls invisibubble.

Easier sneaking-times.

Big mischief!'

Cheers and jumping around in circles followed this speech.

And all this Miranda saw through The Great Magician's crystal ball.

The Great Magician was just about to snap his fingers, and start the kettle boiling for a nice cup of tea, when the Shoes started to glow.

There was a flash and a puff of smoke.

Miranda was gone.

'Oh dear,' said The Great Magician, 'my guests are always doing that.'

CHAPTER 5

The Shoes dropped Miranda out of the sky.

She fell flat on her face and jumped to her feet immediately, pretending it had been a perfect landing, just in case anyone was watching.

Then she looked round to get her bearings.

She was standing on a wooden-slatted bridge over a river, at the bottom of the hill where the castle, and therefore also the trolls' lair, stood.

In her pockets were a sandwich, a bag of marbles and an ancient nail file.

Unfortunately the Shoes had whisked her away from the courtyard of The Great Magician so fast that she had not had time to make a plan.

Before she had time to blink, she was set upon by many small furry things that she now knew to be trolls.

The reason she was set upon by many small furry things,

rather than just the usual two sentries who kept watch for anybody carrying what might pass as food (for, as you know by now, trolls are always hungry) was this: no one knew quite how, but the dragon had got loose in the cave, and was firing jets of flame at anyone who dared to get close enough. It was currently enjoying chasing trolls along the deepest corridors, scorching any rear ends that were not quite fast enough as they ran away.

It was finally 'tamed' temporarily when one of the more insightful members of the little band of trolls threw a bucket of water over its head, both putting its fire out and preventing further flame-throwing.

By the time the dragon had shaken its head free of the bucket, the trolls had pushed it into a cage and chained it to a wall.

In the meantime, however, those not wishing to get in its way, and close enough to a viable exit, had left the cave, suddenly leaving their natural laziness behind and all volunteering for sentry duty for the rest of the day (or at least until the coast was clear).

And so Miranda had been set upon by many trolls, as I said

before, instead of the usual two, and they were a lot more difficult to shake off, there being so many of them and them being so heavy.

Miranda staggered off the bridge, covered in trolls, and sat down. The trolls, not used to a creature giving up a fight so easily, were suspicious at first, but then, smelling the sandwich in Miranda's pocket and deciding to investigate, they ferreted it out and immediately started squabbling over it.

Miranda took this opportunity to run for cover, and as the only cover appeared to be the troll cave, she took a deep breath and plunged into the darkness.

She soon wished she hadn't.

Hundreds of yellow eyes, which, unlike hers, could see in the dark, surrounded her and unseen hands pulled and shoved her deeper and deeper underground until she and the dragon were face-to-face.

The dragon growled and prepared to toast its new acquaintance, but the Silver Shoes flashed menacingly and it gave a snort of surprise and took three steps backwards instead.

The Shoes started to make a series of low clicking noises and the dragon grumbled in reply, but appeared mollified by the end of what appeared to be a conversation and sat down quietly in a corner, watching the Shoes suspiciously out of the corners of its eyes, just in case.

The trolls watched all this with growing excitement as they realised that this new girl-thing with the strangest of feet they had ever laid eyes upon (the trolls, not understanding the concept of shoes, thought that Miranda's were actually her feet) might be able to stop the scorchings they had received previously and not only calm their scaly prisoner, but convince the dragon to work for them, without the need for any extra exertion/work and without the need for any of the trolls to get too close to it.

And so they quickly slammed the door of the cage that the dragon was in, and where now Miranda also stood, and turned the key.

'Oh, great!' thought Miranda. 'What fine mess have you got me into now?'

As if they could hear her thoughts, the Shoes twinkled mischievously.

CHAPTER 6

Miranda spent the next few hours watching the trolls, and they spent the next few hours watching her and pointing and whispering.

Occasionally one would get bored, but would be replaced by another troll.

Then food arrived and there was a fight over who got it and who got the biggest share of it.

When the trolls slept, they fought over the blankets in their sleep, and when any troll was brave enough to stop staring at the new girl-thing in the cave and approached to squeak at her, the rest took the opportunity to pounce on him and start a fight over that.

Miranda eventually realised that fighting each other was like a big game, and that gave her an idea, which became a plan.

She whispered the plan to her Silver Shoes and asked them to communicate it to the dragon.

The Shoes started clicking again, at which point the trolls pricked up their ears and started dancing around and moving closer and looking from girl-thing to dragon and back again.

But when, after a few minutes, nothing happened, the trolls sat back again, all in a row in front of the cage, scratching their heads.

Although the dragon had not reacted to the clicking of the Shoes this time, dragons have notoriously big ears and it heard every click, and it bided its time.

Miranda beckoned to the troll nearest to her. He looked at the other trolls, sitting all in a row.

They all stood up and came right up close to the bars of the cage.

Miranda placed one hand calmly on the head of the first troll and said, 'You're "it".'

The Silver Shoes translated this into troll squeaks, and the rest of the little party, instantly feeling that their companion had been given something special and they hadn't, and they wanted it, crowded round the first troll and a chorus of 'It, it, it . . .' (because that was the only word they could remember and copy themselves) started.

They were so distracted by 'it' that Miranda could easily ask her Silver Shoes to unchain the dragon and open the lock on the cage door, without anyone noticing, and so she did.

Miranda slipped out through the cage door and the Silver Shoes clicked to the dragon, so that it followed her.

The trolls by now had worked out that 'it' could be taken from another person and that you could become 'it' by touching another person, who was 'it'.

They decided that thumping each other was as good a way as any, and so another, much bigger than usual, fight ensued, as more and more trolls became curious at the louder and louder chorus of 'It, it, it, it, it . . .'

As you may imagine, when Miranda and the dragon reached the cave entrance the trolls, not being, perhaps, the most intelligent of creatures, were still fighting over whose turn it was to be 'it'.

As Miranda and the dragon crept out past them and made their escape, one of them tumbled past and out of the hole in the front of the cave, which, as I have mentioned before, was halfway up a hillside, directly overlooking a river.

A splash and a howl of what was a mix of surprise and fury met their ears.

The troll shot back up the hill, faster than a racing ostrich, but flew back past and landed in the river again twice as fast as that.

Miranda suspected that the following morning, when she and the dragon were far away from the tunnels on the hillside, the trolls would be at it still.

The dragon looked round at Miranda with gratitude in its dragon's eyes. It growled a low growl, but this time Miranda did not hear it as a growl. This time she heard it as words, thanks to the power of her magical Shoes.

'Thank you,' it rumbled.

Miranda smiled and the Shoes clicked, 'You're welcome.'

Miranda watched as her dragon rose up over the mound into the sky, with the sunset making its wings glow like fire, and she knew her adventures with the Silver Shoes were only just beginning.

The End